P9-BIY-523

Springtime Treasury

TEMPLAR

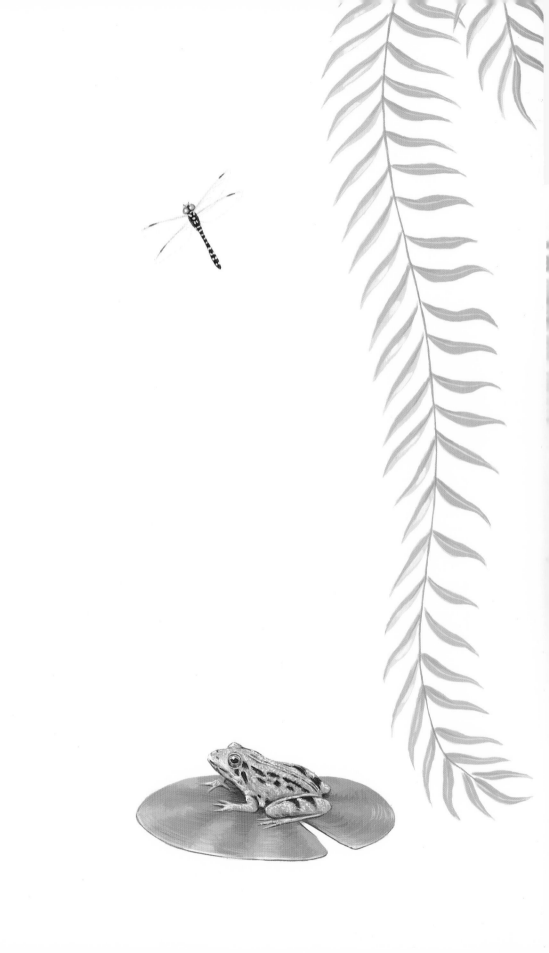

The Little LOST DUCKLING

WRITTEN BY SUE BARRACLOUGH   ILLUSTRATIONS BY SIMON MENDEZ

One sunny morning, Mother Duck led her
four new ducklings down to the old pond.
"Stay close, little ones," she told them.

But one little duckling didn't listen.

"Follow me, my babies," called Mother Duck as she swam away.
But one little duckling didn't do as she was told.
She didn't want to follow her mother across the water.

She wanted to dart after the dragonflies,

... watch the frogs hopping
on the lily pads,

... and chase the glistening fish.

So that's just what Little Duckling did.

She splashed in the water and
frightened the fish. She snapped her
little beak at the dragonflies.
And she quacked in amazement when the
kingfisher flew by, like a little piece
of the summer sky.

After a while, Little Duckling was tired of playing.
She scrambled up onto the riverbank and
fluffed out her feathers to dry.
Around her the wind whispered in the grass.
The leaves rustled, and overhead the sky grew dark.

Little Duckling realized she was all alone.

Little Duckling looked out across the pond.
Mother Duck was nowhere to be seen.
Suddenly, Little Duckling wanted to see
her mother very much indeed.
Just then, Hedgehog came shuffling through the leaves.

"Have you seen my mommy?" asked Little Duckling.
But Hedgehog just shook his head, and carried
on hunting for juicy worms to eat.

So Little Duckling walked a little further
down the riverbank until she met Squirrel.
"Have you seen my mommy?" she asked again.

But Squirrel was too busy collecting acorns
to even answer, so Little Duckling had to
carry on walking.

She hadn't gone very far before she met Rabbit.
"Who are you?" the rabbit asked.
"I'm a lost little duckling and I'm looking for my mommy,"
said Little Duckling bravely.
"Then stay by the water, or Mr. Fox will get you," said
Rabbit. And with a flash of his white tail
he disappeared, back beneath the ground.

Little Duckling wasn't feeling very brave at all now.
She quacked loudly, hoping Mother Duck might hear her.
"I wouldn't do that if I were you," said a squeaky voice.
"Mr. Fox might hear you!" It was Mouse.
"Oh dear, oh dear!" cheeped Little Duckling.
"Please help me find my mommy." But the mouse
had gone, scurrying away through the grass.

Just then, a big, furry beaver scrambled onto the bank.
"Hrrumph!" he grunted. "What's a little duckling
like you doing here, all on your own?

"I'm lost and I'm looking for my mommy!"
wailed the poor little duckling.

"Is she a nice, brown, cuddly mommy?" asked Beaver.
"Who told you always to stay close by her side?"

Little Duckling nodded sadly.
"Then you'll find her looking for YOU over by
those reeds," said Beaver. And so she was.
"...Mommy!"
quacked the little duckling happily,
"I promise to never wander off again."

And do you know what? She never, ever did.

The BLACKBERRY MOUSE

WRITTEN BY MATTHEW GRIMSDALE   ILLUSTRATIONS BY TONY LINSELL

Mouse loved his little cottage in the country.
He loved it because it was warm and cosy,
and just the right size for a mouse.

But most of all, he loved it because there was a BIG blackberry bush in the garden,

and every year he had a bumper crop
of ripe, juicy blackberries.

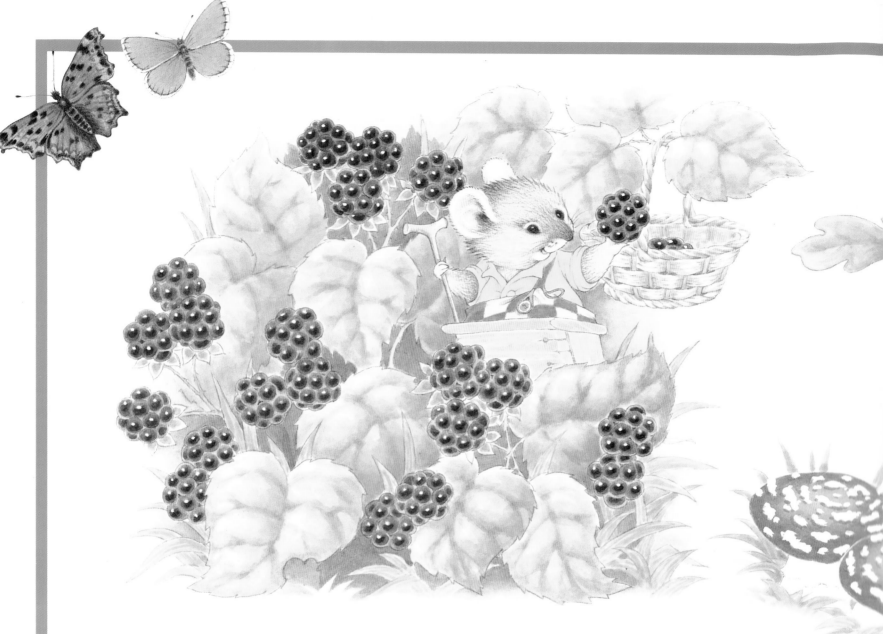

One Summer, Mouse's blackberries were even
bigger and juicier than usual. He began picking right
away and he was already hot and bothered when
Sparrow came by.

"What nice blackberries. May I have some?"
chirped Sparrow.
"They're all mine," said Mouse. "Go away!"
"No need to be rude," said the little bird,
and she flew away.

Mouse's paws were beginning to ache from
all the hard work when he caught sight of Squirrel,
leaning on his garden gate.
"Can I have some of those juicy blackberries?"
Squirrel asked.
"If I give you some then there will be less for me!"
Mouse replied. So Squirrel went away empty-handed.

Mouse had stopped to have a rest when Rabbit
came hopping through the grass.

"Those blackberries look delicious," she said.

"They are," said Mouse. "And I am going to eat every last one."

"Then you will most certainly be ill," said Rabbit,
and off she went.

The sun was hot and Mouse was getting very tired.
Soon he had nodded off to sleep.
He didn't realise that someone had been watching him.

It was Mr. Fox...

When he saw that Mouse was asleep, he sneaked over
Mouse's gate and crept closer and closer until
he could pick up Mouse's basket.

He was just creeping away when
SNAP!
He trod on a twig.

Mouse woke up with a start.
"Hey! Those are my blackberries!" he squeaked.
"You're far too small to stop me taking them,"
laughed Mr. Fox. "They will make a fine dish for my
tea tonight."

Mouse was not surprised that
none of his woodland friends had warned him
Mr. Fox was about that day. "After all," he thought,
"why should they help me when I would not
share my blackberries with them?"

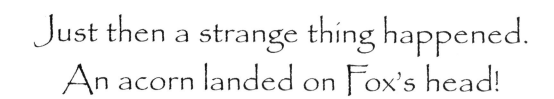

Just then a strange thing happened.
An acorn landed on Fox's head!

PLOP!

and another, PLOP!

and another, and another, and another.

PLOP! PLOP! PLOP!

Mr. Fox dropped the blackberry basket and
ran away as fast as he could!

Mouse looked up to see where the acorns had come from. And who do you think he saw up in the old oak tree?

It was Squirrel and Sparrow, and Rabbit was there too, at the gate.

"We couldn't let Mr. Fox steal your blackberries," said Squirrel. "Even if you didn't want to share them," added Sparrow.

Mouse felt very ashamed. Then he had an idea...

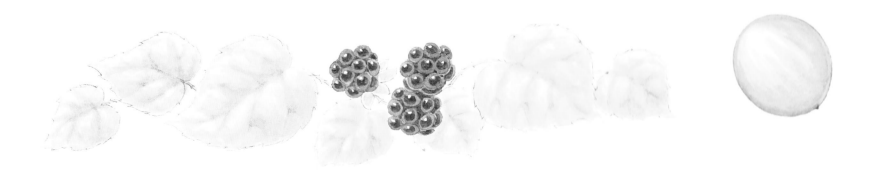

That afternoon Mouse invited everyone to a blackberry feast. He worked all day to get it ready.

There was blackberry juice to drink, blackberry jam, blackberry jelly, blackberry crumble, and lots and lots of little blackberry tarts.
The other animals said how delicious it all was.

"Perhaps," said Mouse, "blackberries are nicer if you share them, after all."

The BUNNY of BLUEBELL HILL

WRITTEN BY TIM PRESTON   ILLUSTRATIONS BY LORNA HUSSEY

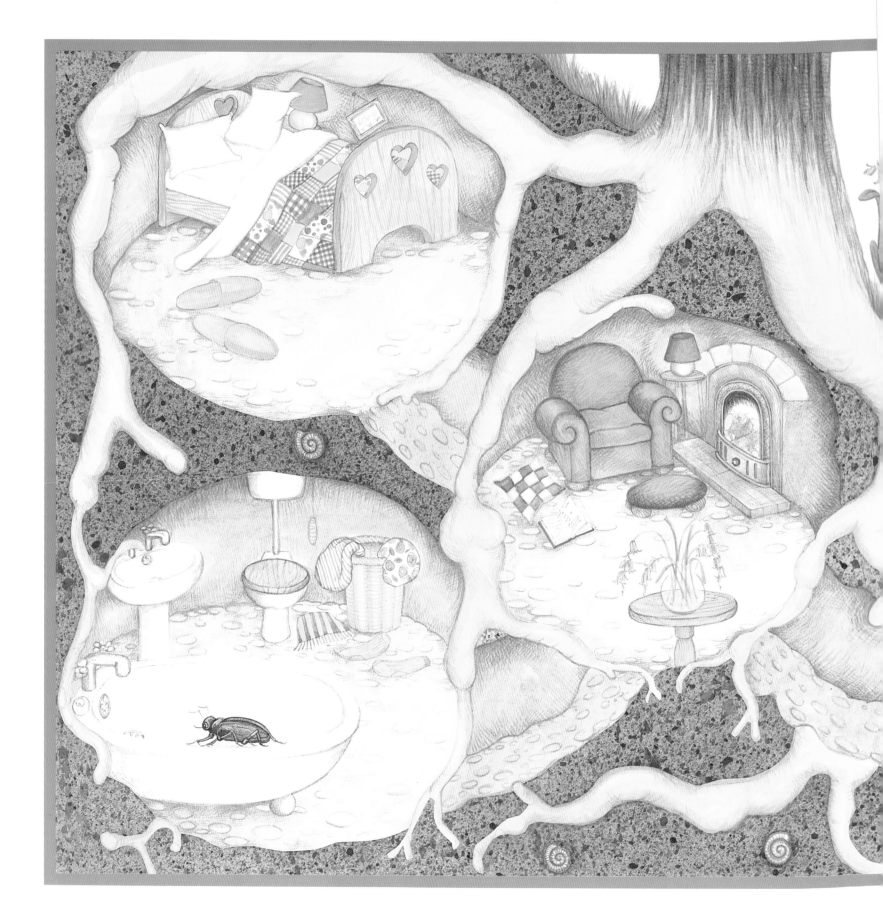

At the top of Bluebell Hill
there was an old oak tree. And underneath
that oak tree there was a burrow,
and in that burrow lived a bunny.
It was a very nice burrow, with four little rooms
and bluebells growing by the front door.

But Bunny didn't like it.

"I am bored with this burrow,"
said Bunny to herself.
"I am tired of walking up and down this hill.
I am fed up with being hit on the head by acorns.
And I am very, very bored with bluebells!

I want an exciting new home."
So without further ado, she
set off to find herself one.

Bunny's friend Squirrel took her to see
his high-rise tree house. But Bunny
didn't have a head for heights!
And her big paws just weren't meant for jumping
about from branch to branch.

"I'm sorry, Squirrel," said Bunny.
"I think I need something a little closer to the ground!"

The next animal Bunny visited was Badger.
He lived in a mossy bank in the heart of the
old forest. It was dark and still among the trees,
and there weren't many passers by,
which was just the way
Badger liked it.

"But it's too quiet for me!" said Bunny.

"If you like company, why not try living by the river?" suggested Otter. "There's always lots going on down here." But Bunny only had to take one look at Otter's houseboat to know that it wouldn't suit her.

"It's much too wet here for me!" she wailed.

"Hmmm, then what about the meadow where Field-mouse lives?" suggested Otter.

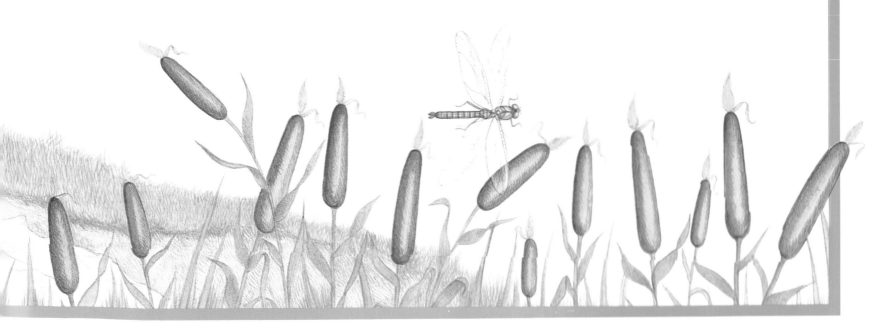

Field-mouse seemed happy living in the meadow,
but no matter how hard she tried, Bunny
just could not get comfortable there.

For a start there was no shade anywhere
and when the sun beat down it was very hot!

And the pollen from the poppies was extremely
sneezy, and the wheat stalks were scratchy.

So that was no good either.

"What about Owl's house?" suggested Field-mouse.
Owl lived in the loft of the old barn.
It was certainly dry, and very clean,
but there was something wrong with that too.
"It's just too drafty," said Bunny.

Would she ever find
a new home?

In the shadow of the mountain the little rabbit
found an empty cave. It was slightly gloomy,
but at least there was lots of space.
She thought it might be just the place, until she heard
a rumbly sound — a low grumbly, growly sort of sound.
Then she realized — it was Bear's house!

"And Bear snores too much," said Bunny.
"I couldn't possibly live near him!"

Bunny was about to give up looking
when she came across a smart blue door amongst
the twisted roots of a chestnut tree.
"This would be perfect!" said Bunny to herself.

But something seemed wrong.
The place had a funny smell —
a frightful, foxy sort of smell...
Suddenly, Bunny felt very afraid and she ran away,
as fast as she could.

Bunny ran and ran, past the barn and the field,
the river and the forest, all the way back to Bluebell Hill.
She ran up the hill, past the bluebells and the oak tree
and straight in through her own front door.

Bunny looked around her little burrow.
"It's not too hot or too wet. It's not too quiet or too noisy.
In fact, it's the perfect place for me!"
said Bunny happily.

And so it was!

A TEMPLAR BOOK

This edition produced in 2003 for Books Are Fun

Devised and produced by The Templar Company plc,
Pippbrook Mill, London Road, Dorking, Surrey RH4 1JE, UK

Copyright © 2003 by The Templar Company plc

All rights reserved

ISBN 1-58209-980-4

Written by Sue Barraclough, Matthew Grimsdale and Tim Preston
Illustrated by Lorna Hussey, Tony Linsell and Simon Mendez
Designed by Hayley Bebb and Caroline Reeves
Edited by Rebecca Beves

Printed in Singapore